THE WATER THIEF
& The Manatee

Kitty Fitzgerald

A Modern Fable

Illustrated by Nicola Balfour

First published 2017 by IRON Press
5 Marden Terrace
Cullercoats
North Shields
NE30 4PD
tel/fax +44(0)191 2531901
ironpress@blueyonder.co.uk
www.ironpress.co.uk

ISBN 978-0-9954579-6-6
Printed by imprintdigital.com

Story © Kitty Fitzgerald
Illustrations © Nicola Balfour
This edition © IRON Press 2017

Book Design Brian Grogan and Peter Mortimer

Typeset in Georgia
IRON Press books are distributed by NBNI International
and represented by Inpress Ltd
Churchill House, 12 Mosley Street,
Newcastle upon Tyne, NE1 1DE
tel: +44(0)191 2308104
www.inpressbooks.co.uk

Me, the Aquatic Ape and the Manatee

I t was at a jumble sale in Derbyshire in 1981 that I first came across the theories of evolutionist, Elaine Morgan. The book was called *The Descent of Woman,* published in 1972 by Souvenir Press. She challenged the traditional – almost entirely male – evolutionary theories with her own bold vision, titled *The Aquatic Ape Theory.*

I had recently been watching a Desmond Morris documentary on evolution and had been neither impressed nor convinced of his arguments. But who was I to challenge him? And yet when I read Morgan's book, it made perfect sense to me. She has since written many other books.

Establishment male evolutionists ridiculed her work for decades until their theory about our move from four to two legs was shown to be inaccurate. Last year, David Attenborough said publicly that acknowledgement of and recognition for Morgan's theories was well overdue.

Water is essential for humans and creatures of all kinds. We need to protect it from those who pollute it, from those who prevent access to others and those who want to sell it to the highest bidder.

The Aquatic Ape theory was first proposed by the marine biologist Alister Hardy in 1960. The Manatee belongs to the scientific order, Sirenia. All sirenian species in the world are listed as endangered or vulnerable by the IUCN – World Conservation Union. www.savethemanatee.org

Kitty Fitzgerald *Cullercoats, Summer 2017*

Photo Mik Critchlow

KITTY FITZGERALD has written five well-received novels: *Identity* (Room to Write 2014), *Pigtopia* (Faber & Faber), *Small Acts of Treachery* (Brandon), *Snapdragons* (Brandon) *Marge* (Sheba) and a collection of short stories, *Miranda's Shadow* (IRON Press 2013) She has been published in 24 countries. She took 2nd place (fiction) in the *Barnes & Noble Discover Award* and has written for radio drama and theatre. Her writing awards include: *Hawthornden Fellowship, Hosking House Fellowship, Henrich Boll Award*. In Autumn 2015, she was Writer in Residence at the Centre for Creative Writing and Oral Culture, University of Manitoba, Canada. She is currently working on another fable and her first crime novel. Kitty comments that working with the illustrator Nicola Balfour has been great fun.

NICOLA BALFOUR is an artist educator living in Easington Colliery, County Durham. She moved from The New Forest to Newcastle in 1981 where she studied Fine Art at the then Newcastle Poly. She was the art editor for IRON Press for a brief but happy time and has helped design and paint miles of silk banners with countless community and school groups. She has been a pantomime camel, environmental artist, a creative agent and is the proud mother of 2 daughters. She is a co-director at The Barn at Easington, an outdoor arts and education centre. The Water Thief is her third book illustration. 'It's been a really joyful experience to work with Kitty who has given me the space and freedom to create.'

Contents

		Page
Chapter 1	The Manatee	7
Chapter 2	The Child	17
Chapter 3	Changes	29
Chapter 4	What has happened to the water?	39
Chapter 5	Into the mountain caves	49
Chapter 6	What will they do?	61

The Water Thief and the Manatee

Tomas felt compassion and something else that he didn't understand.

1.
The Manatee

Tomas was a fisherman who lived alone in a small house close to the sea. For generations his family had fished from little boats, riding the waves like dolphins. One soft, spring day he started building a new wall to protect his home from the encroaching waves. After a few hours, he sat on a rock to rest, thinking it was strange how the place he'd lived in all his life had this curious relationship with water. On one side of the town was the unpredictable sea, which ate away at a little more of the land with every tide, while the rest of the area was dry and dusty.

Tomas glanced at his blue and yellow boat lazing peacefully in the bay. As he daydreamed and just before his eyes completely closed, he thought he heard a sweet voice calling,

'Come to me...come, but don't come too close.'

It was the sort of voice that might belong to a rainbow. He was intrigued and opened his eyes. He couldn't see anyone so he followed the sound. Near the back of his boat, by the lapping water, he discovered a female manatee in the shallows. Her paddle tail was caught up in an old oil barrel and some wire mesh so that she was unable to swim properly. His first thought was to ignore her; but when he looked into the creature's eyes, he remembered what his mother had said to him when he was nine years old and preparing for his first fishing trip with his older brother.

'Manatees are special creatures, some think them sacred, keep clear of them with the boat and the nets.'

As he stared at the manatee, Tomas felt compassion and something else that he didn't understand. The emotion rose up in him so strongly that it frightened him.

'Don't be afraid, I'm hurt but I won't harm you,' the manatee said.

Tomas was startled because she didn't open her mouth to speak like he did but somehow her words slipped into his mind.

It was then that Tomas noticed the cuts on the

creature's back and saw the glistening fragments of steel sticking out from her side. He knew what had happened; the creature had been hit by at least one speedboat. The boat engines had a low frequency, which meant the manatee couldn't hear them coming because her hearing was in the high range. She must have been right out to the channel, over six miles away, because pleasure boats were rare around his area. Although, when he thought about it, he realized he'd recently seen many more of them crossing the bay.

'Will you help me?' the manatee asked.

Tomas knew at once that he would. He stepped closer.

'Be careful,' the manatee said. 'You must never touch my skin with your bare hands.'

'Why not?'

'If I tell you, you won't believe me.'

'Try me,' he said.

'Because if you do, for a brief time, I'll turn into a woman and you'll fall in love with me.'

Tomas laughed.

'You see,' the manatee said, 'you think it's not true but it is.'

Tomas laughed again.

'It is true,' she said. 'Your kind and mine share a long story; we have been close on land and sea for thousands of years.'

'Ridiculous,' Tomas said.

He'd heard many stories about sea creatures that were supposed to lure men to some island and he knew that manatees were often mistaken for these mythical beasts. He turned away from her and pulled a long rope from inside the boat to tie around her body. He attached it to the wooden jetty, so that she wouldn't be pulled away into deeper waters. When she was secure he fetched seaweed and turtle grass for her to eat.

Day after day after day, he nursed the manatee back to health, untangling her tail, cleaning the wounds and feeding her, but he always wore his strong gloves for protection. And every day she told him more stories about humans and sea creatures:

'From our skins you can make medicines to heal yourselves and you don't have to kill us to do it. That is because we lived together in the sea for so long that it shaped us to help each other. Even when you left the sea, so many years ago, we would rescue you...like when you battled hard ice and fell through, we pushed you out of the ice tomb. But later, when you started to kill us...things changed.'

'I thought we always killed you,' said Tomas.

'No...no...long times back, we were companions in

the sea, co-operating with each other against other huge creatures that swallowed everything in their path.'

Tomas shook his head and sighed.

'It all sounds strange to me,' he said.

Ten days later, when the manatee was well and preparing to return to the sea, Tomas was overcome with a sadness he'd never before experienced. In his boat, he followed the rolling, diving creature a long way out. As she came alongside the boat for the last time, Tomas couldn't help himself.

'Please don't leave,' he said and on impulse, reached down to touch her glistening back. A feeling, like electricity, shivered up his arm and when he looked into the water, the manatee was gone and a woman swam alongside the boat. He reached down, helped her on board and wrapped her in his coat.

'Is it you?' he asked.

'Yes, it's me,' she said. 'But I can only stay like this for a short while.'

'I can't believe it.'

Stars sparkled in her eyes and her skin had the turquoise sheen of fish scales. Tomas took his boat back to shore and led her to his house where he lit a huge fire to keep her warm. He found clothes that would fit her and turned away as she dressed.

'Are you hungry?' he asked.

'Some greens please.'

'Is that all?'

'It's what I like.'

'I'm not sure you're well enough to go back home... oh, do you live in one place?'

'We used to have an area that was ours and from there we often travelled to visit other colonies...but now...we generally live alone.'

'So do I,' said Tomas, 'and it can get lonely.'

'Have you heard about the strangers who have come to the mainland and some of the other bays? They are building lots of houses.'

'I heard something but there's enough room for all of us, isn't there?'

She stared into his eyes and Tomas saw a shadow pass across hers.

'They're not fishermen like you, Tomas. They have large, noisy boats and huge nets, that would cover this whole bay. And they have fast motorboats that hurt us.'

'I'm sure we'll all find a way to live together,' said Tomas.

They sat and ate and talked about their lives. Tomas couldn't stop grinning. She made his small house seem snug and homely; her laughter filled every corner of the room.

'Please tell me more about the sea,' he said.

She told him old tales about the strange things buried in the depths of the ocean.

'It's a beautiful world. Whole villages and towns, statues and ceramics, buried beneath the waves,' she said. 'Did you know that mountains rise up from the floor of the sea? Some ridges run for thousands of miles.'

'I didn't know that but I'd like to see all these things,' said Tomas.

'They're deep down in the sea; your lungs have changed since you left us and you'd find it hard to travel to that depth. But perhaps I will take you one day and help you breathe. It's a glorious sight and it will be somewhere in your old memories, Tomas: all the wonder that's beneath the sea.'

'Why would it be in my memory?'

'I told you, because your kind once lived there with us; there are ancient paintings of us together, on cavern walls underneath the sea.'

Tomas shook his head, 'No, that can't be true. How could we breathe?'

'It was a long time back but don't human babies have small fins before they are born? Don't they live and breathe in fluid in their mother's wombs?'

Tomas shook his head. 'I have no children; I know nothing about that.'

'Because we lived in the sea together, your females have watery birth sacs to bring their offspring to their time. Over the centuries, the stories have been passed down to us. The earth had a time when it was scorching hot…that is when you came out of the trees and caves and into the sea with us.'

'This is all too new and complex for me,' Tomas said. 'My head is spinning.'

The manatee laughed; it was like birdsong. Tomas grinned so much his face hurt.

When darkness came, they walked along the beach and watched the moonlight playing with the sea. Tomas put his extra coat down on the sand and they lay side by side, pointing out special stars to each other. Later, she kissed him softly and Tomas felt a passion he'd never before experienced. The woman rested her head on his chest and sighed. They soon fell asleep.

As dawn tickled his eyelids, Tomas sat up and looked around. Both of his coats covered him and had kept the cold out all night, but the woman was gone. He ran to edge of the sea and saw her waving.

She was a long way out and with a flash of silver she disappeared into the ocean. Tomas waited for her to surface and when she didn't, he got into his boat and rowed out to the last place he'd seen her. There he sat, for hours and hours, calling to her, begging her to return. But it was no use and he had to set off back to his house without her.

That night, as he lay restless in his bed, unable to forget the manatee-woman, he dreamed he stood by the seashore. Out of the waves walked the woman, luminous against the steel blue of the ocean. She smiled at him and when he touched her, his fingers sparked with heat and small silver shapes bounced off her skin. She took hold of his hand and led him into the sea, down into the depths where it was darker than the deepest night. She kept him warm with her arms and breathed life into his lungs as they tumbled and turned in the water. And just when he thought he would never breathe fresh air again, she pulled him up into an underground cavern lit by hundreds of strange fish whose bodies glowed like fire. There, on the cave walls, she showed him paintings of humans, manatees and other sea creatures living together in the oceans.

All night long, Tomas lay beside her, talking and laughing. When morning came, she gently pulled him back into the sea and up to the bay. As she plunged back into the water, Tomas shouted for her to stay but when she dropped into the ocean, he saw that she'd changed back into the manatee.

When Tomas woke up in his own bed, alone, disappointment flashed through his whole body. But when he pulled back his bedcovers, to go and look out of his window, he discovered the sheets were damp and tiny tendrils of silver seaweed clung to his legs.

2.
The Child

DAYS, WEEKS, MONTHS PASSED; TIME IN WHICH Tomas worked hard to try and forget his experience with the sea woman; to forget her arms around him and to forget her laughter. Each day he went out in his boat to catch fish to sell in the town marketplace and every minute of every day he yearned to hear the manatee calling him. Eventually, sadness settled around his heart and often, the pain of it made him shiver.

Exactly one year from the night she left, Tomas was woken by her sweet voice.
   'Tomas,' she called. 'Tomas, come quickly.'

In between Tomas and the manatee, a baby floated on the tail of a dolphin.

He rushed out of bed and down to the water's edge. By the light of a full, amber moon he saw her. She was rolling and turning in the sea a little way from the shore. He jumped in and swam out. As he reached her and before he could touch her, everything became silent and still, until the sound of a crying baby rang out. By the light of the moon, Tomas followed the sound and there, in between him and the manatee, a baby floated on the tail of a dolphin.

With her nose, the manatee nudged the baby towards Tomas. He picked the infant up in his arms and knew, without any doubt, that this was his part-manatee, part-human girl child.

'She's beautiful,' he said.

The manatee nodded. She leant over the baby and whispered into her ears, sounds that Tomas had never before heard.

'You must raise our child,' the manatee said. 'She is more human than manatee. Will you take care of her and love her?'

'Gladly,' said Tomas, as he held the baby close to his chest. 'But will we ever see you again?'

'Perhaps.' She brushed his face gently with her flipper and was gone, heading out into the vastness of the ocean.

Some unfathomable instinct, like a quiet voice always inside his head, told Tomas what he needed to do to raise the child. He told the neighbours he was fostering her for friends who'd died suddenly.
He called her Maria, an ancient name for the sea.

Over the years, Maria grew tall and strong and knew nothing of her real mother, but in the spaces between her fingers and toes, she sometimes thought she could feel the soft filigree of webbing and she always had a longing to be close to the sea. Whenever Maria asked questions about her real parents, Tomas made up stories and then he'd forget what he'd said. He daren't tell her the truth because he was afraid that she'd leave him and go off into the ocean. Maria noticed that Tomas never told the same story twice. Yet something told her that one day she'd discover the truth.

She went fishing with Tomas and learned his skills: How to handle the small boat and how to catch fish so that they were constantly renewed. When she said she wanted to go to school and learn everything there was to know about the world, he didn't argue. He knew she had brains to burn.

When she was twelve years old, Maria began to have the same dream over and over again. In it she swam with dolphins, whales, manatees and sang the songs they taught her. They carried her on their backs into the depths of the ocean and often she thought she heard a voice calling her name. Sometimes her dreams were so real that her bed was damp and sandy and she found small pebbles and shells on her bedroom floor. When she told her father about her vivid dreams he tried to distract her by saying,

'Do you think you're a fish?'

And Maria would reply,

'In my dreams I'm like a fish, diving in the dark, deep sea.'

When Maria wasn't dreaming about the sea or going to school, she swam in the ocean, hour after hour after hour. Tomas worried more and more about losing her and became cross and bad tempered.

'Come here you lazy girl!' he'd shout. 'Come and fetch water from the well. Come and make yourself useful.'

Afterwards, he'd be angry with himself for shouting at her and he'd smother her with affection.

Nobody in the region had ever thought much about the well that stood at the foot of the mountains. It had always been there and that was that. However, when Maria was seventeen and finished with school, on a certain day she went to the well and discovered that the level of the water had gone way down. It took her twice as long as it usually did to fill the buckets.

When she got home, Maria told her father about the well but he said she was just daydreaming. So, from then on, every time Maria went to fill their buckets she made a mark on the side of the wall to show the level of the water. And every week, without fail, the water got less and less.

In a land that has no rain, a well with no water is a disaster. When it's the only well in the town, it's a major catastrophe.

'Tomas,' she called out one day as she reached home.

'What is it?' he asked as he came running from the back of the house where he'd been chopping wood.

'The level of the water in the well is very low.'

'It goes up and down with the seasons,' he said.

'If that's true, why have I never noticed it?'

Tomas thought for a moment. 'Maybe I'm wrong; we'll keep and eye on it from now on.'

'I have been doing that. I've been putting a mark at the level of water for days and days. You must come

and see for yourself.'
'I will...I will.'

The following day, Maria was unable to reach down to mark the level of the water. That afternoon, she persuaded Tomas to go and inspect the well. When he did, he got a terrible shock. There was a huge high fence around it with a sign saying: KEEP OUT.

'Keep out?' Tomas shouted. 'Keep out? Who the devil thinks they can stop us from having our water?'

'I do,' said a voice behind him.

He looked around and saw a striking young man, with long hair and a decorative hat, on horseback. The man trotted around the well and around Tomas before dismounting.

'Pleased to meet you,' he said.

'Well,' said Tomas. 'If this is your fence and your notice, then I'm sorry I can't say the same.'

'It belongs to my family. It's our land and it's our water,' said the stranger.

'What is your family name?' asked Tomas.

'You can call me Sebastian.'

Tomas stared at him for a few moments.

'You won't tell me your family name; why is that?'

'Like I said, please call me Sebastian.'

'Well then, Sebastian, how come this is now your

well? It has belonged to our people for generations upon generations.'

Sebastian reached into his bag and drew out a roll of paper, which he unfurled with a flourish. 'By Legal Declaration, the well is mine. See for yourself,' he said.

Tomas couldn't read the language of the city but he didn't want the stranger to know that, so he called for Maria, who'd learned it at school. But when he saw the way the stranger looked at her - like a shark at a shaking leg - he wished he'd left her at home.

As he introduced himself to Maria, the stranger took hold of her hand and kissed it. 'Sebastian, at your service,' he said.

Maria laughed but Tomas scowled. He pointed at the declaration and said to her,

'See what that says.'

Maria carefully read the document but every so often she couldn't resist a glance at the stranger. She'd never seen anyone like him. Each time she looked his way, he blew her a kiss.

As Maria finished reading, Tomas drew her to one side to find out what she'd learned.

'It does say that he and his people have been given the land with the well and they now control the water.'

'From today, people must pay for the water they use,' said Sebastian.

'By whose orders?' Tomas asked.

'The International Consortium for Continual Development.'

'Nonsense! Who are they? I've never heard of them,' said Tomas. 'People around here won't stand for this: it's theft.'

'I believe,' said Sebastian, 'that you're mistaken. They have no choice; the land and the well now belong to my family. You have had generations of free water and now you will have to pay for it, like everyone else.'

'But how is this possible? How are you allowed to take our land and our water just when the water is becoming scarce?' Tomas said.

'I will control the water supply and ration it out so that nobody goes without and you'll pay me for looking after it.'

Sebastian nodded and turned his attention to Maria.

'Are your free this afternoon?' he said.

'No, she isn't,' said Tomas.

'Yes, I am,' said Maria.

'Then I would very much like to take you out for a picnic.'

'No,' said Tomas.

'Yes,' said Maria.

'But you have chickens to feed and wood to chop,' said Tomas.

Maria frowned.

'Come,' said Sebastian to Maria. 'We will do your jobs together before we go for a ride and a picnic.' He turned to Tomas, 'all right old man?'

Before Tomas could reply, Sebastian lifted Maria on to the back of his horse and rode towards the bay.

Tomas was shocked. Maria had never before disobeyed him. His heart beat irrationally and he stayed where he was and grumbled to himself. He didn't like being called an old man either.

He sat on a rock and listened to the thud, thud of wood being chopped and the clacking of hens being fed and his stomach felt sick at the thought of losing the well and even worse, maybe losing his daughter. He had never thought beyond Maria's childhood and now he had to accept that she was a lovely young woman.

When the work was finished, Sebastian – with Maria behind him on the horse, her arms around his waist – slowly walked the beast in front of Tomas who sat in front of the house.

'Have a rest, Tomas,' Maria called out. I'll see you later. I'll be fine.'

'You bring her home safely, or else… ' Tomas shouted.

Sebastian rode off without responding.

Tomas watched them disappear up the mountain track and discovered that his eyes had filled with tears. He felt lost, abandoned and he didn't know what to do.

Slowly, Maria was charmed by Sebastian's stories.

3.
Changes

Forty minutes later, Sebastian stopped his horse and helped Maria down. He produced, from saddlebags resting each side of the beast, wonderful cheese, caraway seed buns, fresh tomatoes and basil leaves drizzled with oil and balsamic vinegar. He spread a rug on the ground, set the feast out and sat down. He patted the space beside him.

'Come, Maria…rest and eat.'

Maria tried a bit of everything and smiled at him.

'This is all so delicious. Thank you. Now you must tell me about yourself. Where do you live? When did you come to this area? '

'I live up in the mountains but I am much more interested in hearing about you; your dreams, your passions...'

She leaned back on her elbows and sighed. 'Well, I have a dream; that one day I will be a great swimmer.'

'How far can you swim before you get tired?'

'Oh, miles and miles.'

'In the sea?'

'Of course, where else?'

He laughed. 'Have you never seen a swimming pool?'

'On films we sometimes see at the town hall, but not round here.'

'But we have them in the mountains.'

'I don't think so.'

Sebastian nodded. 'Yes, Maria and one day I will take you to see for yourself. You can swim faster in a pool; there are no waves and it's warmer.'

'How does the water come in and out then?'

Sebastian laughed. 'You are so sweet...come, I have chocolate for us.'

Tomas sat for hours and worried. He forgot about drinking or eating. Did this stranger want his daughter as well as the water? She was seventeen and could legally make up her own mind. He was so upset he went into town and tried hard to persuade the people to refuse to pay for the water and to make a stand. But apart from a few, they refused.

'But if we let a stranger steal our water,' Tomas argued. 'What will he steal next? Our land, our houses, our daughters?'

'It's all right for you,' the mayor said, 'you make your living in the sea but these people need water for crops and all sorts of other things. We can't afford to antagonize this man.'

'We should challenge his claim to the water, at least.'

'And how would we do that? Do you know any lawyers? And if one of us did, how would we pay for an investigation and a court case? You're not thinking straight, Tomas.'

Every day, Tomas became more and more angry about the water and every day Maria spent more and more time with Sebastian. He fascinated her. He took her riding on his horse; he offered her delicious, exotic food to eat; he told her stories about the city; about moving staircases; glass towers; dancing and singing in the streets; cafés that were open all night long, marvellous travelling shows from all over the world and swimming pools.

Slowly, Maria was charmed by Sebastian's stories and by his enthusiasm and she had no time for dreaming and swimming. She forgot the songs she'd learned and her mother, the manatee, swam alone in the ocean, calling out her name, but Maria didn't hear. She came home late at night and went out again before breakfast and Tomas remembered what it had been like without Maria, how lonely he'd been. He didn't know what to do because she didn't want to listen to his complaints.

Because he was frightened of losing her, Tomas grew more and more furious about the stranger. All his savings were used up to buy fresh water and he waited up every night for Maria to get home, safely. But one night when she returned, he complained.

'How can you be so friendly to this stranger who has taken our water?'

'But he's doing it for our own good,' Maria said.

'For our own good, what nonsense.'

'No it's not. We were just using the water as if it would be there forever.'

'It will always be there,' Tomas said.

'Nothing lasts forever,' Maria replied.

'Bah,' said Tomas. 'Bah, bah, bah.'

'You sound like a bad tempered goat,' Maria said,

'Look how happy he makes me; why can't you be pleased? I bet my real parents would be.'

She left him stomping his feet on the ground to disguise how much her comment hurt him. He wanted to shout out: 'I am your father,' but some instinct told him he shouldn't.

The next morning, when Sebastian saw that Maria was sad, he pulled her into his arms.

'What's wrong, my lovely chick?'

She shook her head.

'Please, tell me.'

'Tomas is so angry...with you about the water and with me, for being with you.'

'Well Maria, I want you to forget about all that because today, I have a surprise for you,' he said.

She laughed and held her hand out.

'It's too big to hold in your hands,' he said. 'I have to show you.'

He took her for a long ride on his horse, up into the mountains where she'd never been. When he stopped and helped her off the horse, he made her close her eyes while he led her by the hand.

'Now,' Sebastian said, 'turn around three times, snap your fingers twice and open your eyes.'

Maria did as he said and when she opened her

eyes, she was inside an amazing cavern all lit up with phosphorous lamps. Laid out on the stone slabs was a fantastic feast of fresh mangoes, pineapples, blueberries and freshly whipped ice cream in ten different colours.

Maria was so pleased she hugged Sebastian and he danced her around the cavern and sang:

Maria, I've just met a girl called Maria…

'You're so good to me,' she said.

'That's because you are my beautiful chickadee.'

He took hold of her hand and led her to sit on some decorative rugs and together they ate the feast he'd prepared.

When they'd finished eating, he took hold of her hand and said,

'Would you like to live with me on a hill, overlooking the sea, my little cherubim?'

'But I don't know where you live,' Maria said. 'Can we go for a visit?'

He turned away for a second before responding.

'Soon, there are still things to be done to my house. And when it's finished, you will be able to swim in my fantastic pool any time of the day or night, the water is so clean and pure.'

'How do you make the seawater so clean and pure?' she asked.

'Oh...I...there's a special process. I'm having the machinery shipped in.'

'Really? Could it make the seawater as pure as drinking water?'

'I... oh no, no, we could never get it that pure.'

'That's a shame because it would solve the water problem and make Tomas happy.'

'It's just not possible my sweet.'

Down by the sea, Tomas unloaded his fish, gutted them and hung them in the cold larder next to the smoke room. Later, he walked up and down the shoreline, thinking. He wanted Maria back. The stranger had taken her away from him and he had nobody to talk to. He missed her laughter and her singing. And as he thought about the songs she used to sing, he remembered the manatee; she was Maria's mother, maybe she could help.

Tomas turned towards the sea. The sun was just going down, making elegant light patterns on the surface of the water. He called to the manatee,

'Come to me, come to me, come to me soon,' he shouted. Over and over again he called out. 'Come to me, come to me, come to me soon,' until his voice was nothing more than a crackly whisper. Then he fell to his knees on the sand and cried. He stayed there long after the sun had gone and the moon glimmered playfully on the sea. He was so exhausted he finally fell asleep on the sand, curled up like a cat.

As the darkness grew, Maria and Sebastian rode slowly down the side of the mountain. She put her arms around him and rested her head on his back. The motion of the horse almost sent her to sleep. When they reached the small house by the ocean, he helped her down and got down on one knee.

'What are you doing?' she asked.

'I'm going to ask you to be my wife and share my life and have lots of little chicklingtons with me.'

'Are you serious? I mean, maybe I don't want lots of chicklingtons.'

Sebastian frowned. 'Is there something you want more?'

Maria dropped her head back and looked up at the sky.

'Travel,' she said.

'Where to?'

'I want to travel on the sea, around the world. Tomas has an old atlas and we've worn the pages out looking at it, week after week for as long as I can remember.'

'So...if you could travel, which places would you like to visit?'

She closed her eyes and when she opened them

again, he thought he saw the ocean in them. He took a step back.

'Venezuela, Iceland, Hudson Bay, Alaska, the Scottish Islands, Ireland, Lebanon, the Ivory Coast, Mali, the Punjab...' Sebastian put his hand over her mouth.

'Maria, you are so beautiful,' he said.

He put his hand in his pocket and pulled out a ring with a large blue stone.

'Please marry me,' he said, 'and together we will travel before we have lots of chicklingtons...how does that sound?

Maria put the ring on her finger and jumped up and down with joy. 'Yes! Yes, I will marry you,' she shouted.

Sebastian picked her up and whirled her round and round until she was dizzy.

'What about Tomas? Would you like me to come with you to tell him?'

Maria thought for a moment before saying,

'No, let me tell him, quietly, on my own.'

Sebastian nodded, kissed her on the cheek, climbed onto his horse and rode away into the night.

There was still no water.

4.
What has happened to the water?

MARIA RAN TO FIND TOMAS. SHE SEARCHED every room in the house but there was no sign of him. She picked up a lantern and went to see if his boat was there; sometimes he did go night fishing. She wanted to tell him her good news. When she found him, curled up in a tight ball on the sand and shivering with the cold, she was shocked. He looked so small and thin. She shook him.

'Tomas…Tomas…wake up,' she said but she couldn't stir him. The air around her was suddenly dense and thick, as a fret crept in from the sea.

'Tomas! Please, Tomas, wake up!'

The salt on her tongue made her gag and she thought she was going to be sick. She pulled with all her strength until she had Tomas on his feet and then she pulled and dragged him back to the house.

She lowered him onto the sofa, covered him with rugs, piled wood on the dying fire and pushed at the bellows to spark it into life. Once it was blazing, she picked up the kettle and went to fill it with water. In the store cupboard, the water buckets were empty, except for one and that only held only enough for one mug of tea.

When the tea was ready, she lifted Tomas' head and tried to spoon it into his dry mouth.

'Come on Tomas, please, you must wake up,' she said softly.

Very slowly his eyelids began to quiver, blink and then open. He stared at her for a moment as if he wasn't sure who she was.

'What happened? I found you shivering on the beach.'

For a moment, he considered telling her the truth about her mother but again decided it wasn't the right time.

He yawned and stretched. 'I went down to check the boat and I must have fallen asleep.'

'Are you sure you're all right?'

'Yes, I'm fine, just a bit tired.' He stroked her hand. 'I miss having you around as well.'

Maria decided it wasn't a good time to tell him about Sebastian's proposal.

'There's no water in the cupboard,' she said.

Tomas started to get up. 'I'll go to the well. Have you got any money?'

Maria frowned. 'I've never known you without money,' she said.

He sighed. 'It's the water; it mounts up when you have to pay for it every day.'

He was exhausted and his voice was weaker than usual. 'You stay there and rest, I'll go and get water,' Maria said.

She went up to her room, counted out enough money to fill two buckets, fetched the flashlight and walked to the well.

The mechanical door that gave access to the well, only allowed one bucket to be filled each time. So she had to go in and out and then in again. As she waited for her second entry to the well, she thought about her wedding to Sebastian. What would she wear? Where would they have the reception? Who would she invite? When she got access, she threw the bucket down the well but there was no splash. She pulled it back up and it was empty. She tried again and still there was no water.

A few other people had gathered to get water and they became restless.

'Hurry up,' Bella the baker shouted. 'I have to get my bread finished.'

'There's no water,' said Maria as she came through the fence. The gate clanged shut behind her.

'Are you sure?' asked Bella.

'Absolutely, there's no water.'

Bella the baker turned to the person behind her and said, 'There's no water.' And that person turned to the one behind him and said, 'There's no water.' And all along the line of people waiting, the shout went: 'There's no water.' Until the noise was so loud that Maria had to bang her buckets together to shut everybody up.

'Perhaps it needs time fill up again,' she said. 'Maybe in the morning the well will be full.'

'Perhaps? Maybe? That's not good enough,' Bella the baker said. 'People have a living to make. My bread will be spoiled if I don't get water.' Bella said. 'This never happened before we had to pay for it. Go and ask that boyfriend of yours what he's going to do about it.'

'Yes, go and ask him,' others shouted.

'But...I...I don't know where he lives,' Maria said.

'You don't know where your boyfriend lives? And you've been running about with him for months and months. What sort of carry on is that?' Bella shouted.

'I'll go at first light,' Maria said. She turned to Bella the baker and took her hand.

'I promise you I'll find out what's happened by tomorrow. Have some of my water now, for your bread.' She poured half of her bucket of water into Bella's.

There was a moment while they all stared at her, before Bella turned to the crowd and shouted,

'Be here tomorrow, she'll get water for us.'

She turned back to Maria. 'We will be here...you tell that man of yours. He said he would look after the water and now look. It's not good enough. We should have listened to Tomas; we should have fought for our water.'

Others close by joined in, saying,

'We should all have listened to Tomas.'

They reluctantly drifted away and Maria ran back to the little house by the ocean. She was confused. Why did they all blame her? Sebastian was trying to help them to look after the water. Why didn't they understand that?

When she got home, Tomas wasn't in the house.

Her heart did a somersault at the thought he might have fallen and hurt himself. She ran to the beach and found him standing in the sea up to his knees and calling:

'Come to me...come to me...come soon.'

She ran up to him and tried to pull him out of the water but he didn't want to move. 'What are you doing?' she asked.

Tomas didn't know what to say.

'Listen, Tomas, you have to help me. The well is dry and I've promised the townspeople I'll find Sebastian and make sure they have water for early morning.'

He stared at her for a moment as if he didn't understand what she wanted and then his eyes seemed to focus properly.

'Take one of the donkeys. They can climb right to the top of the mountains.'

'But...but I don't know where he lives.'

Tomas was shocked. His mouth fell open.

'You don't know where Sebastian lives? Well, where has he been taking you? I thought you were meeting his parents. I thought you were safe.'

'I was safe. Sebastian wouldn't hurt me. He's asked me to marry him.'

'He's asked you to marry him and you haven't met his family? That's not good.'

Maria turned away from Tomas for a moment and then turned back and shouted,

'You never liked him did you? You never trusted him. You don't care about my happiness.'

'Yes I do, Maria. I care more about your happiness than I do my own. But this man has come here and taken our water and now he wants to take you.'

Maria was so angry and frustrated, she pushed Tomas and he fell backwards into the sea. But just before he went under the water, he was pushed up and on to the beach by the manatee. And when he saw her he shouted with joy.

'You came... you came...thank you...' And without thinking, he threw his arms around her head and the manatee slipped back into the water.

After a few breathless seconds, the water rippled and out came the woman. Tomas pulled his coat off and wrapped it around her. He took her hand and led her to Maria, who was in a state of shock.

'Maria,' Tomas said quietly, 'this is your mother.'

Maria hesitated before she fell into the woman's arms. With a great whoosh of emotion, she realized how long it had been since she'd swum in the sea or dreamed of swimming with the manatee.

'The dreams, the songs, the swimming...it was you,' she said.

'It was me, looking out for you. I only have a short time as a woman and there's so much I have to say.'

Maria looked into her eyes, as if she was searching for answers to questions she hadn't yet thought of; she saw herself there as a tiny baby being born into the sea and how the manatee nudged her into her Tomas's arms. She looked at him with a question in her eyes.

'Yes, I'm your father,' he said and Maria laughed and cried at the same time. The three of them wrapped their arms around each other and stood like that for almost five minutes, sighing and laughing, before separating to walk back to the house.

As they sat around the fire, drinking sea buckthorn wine, Tomas shone with happiness. The manatee-woman had answered his call and Maria now knew he was her father. He glanced at Maria, who still looked troubled.

'Don't worry, Maria,' he said. 'We'll find a way to get some water for the townspeople.'

'You don't have water?' the manatee woman said.

'Our well has run dry,' said Maria.

'But...I don't understand. Up in the mountains they have lots of water. Fountains, swimming pools and now another marina is being built and we manatees are worried the pleasure boats will destroy us all.'

'Is that where Sebastian lives?' Tomas asked Maria.

'No, it can't be, Sebastian would never waste water like that when we are desperate for it here in the valley. You just don't know him.'

'Who is Sebastian?' The woman asked.

'He's asked Maria to marry him.'

Maria glanced at her father. 'But father doesn't trust him. How far away is all this water?' she asked her mother.

'Come, I'll show you. We can swim through the mountains.'

'But it's late, wait until tomorrow,' said Tomas.

'We can't wait, father...we have to get water for the town. They will all be waiting in the morning and we have no water left in the house.'

'Will you come back with Maria?' Tomas asked the manatee.

The woman shook her head. 'It's time to go,' she said.

'But you stayed longer, before.'

'That's only allowed once in a life. After that the change gets shorter every time, until it can't ever be done again.'

He nodded and tried to smile. The woman hugged him and he breathed in her scent, an intoxicating mix off civet, cloves and brine, which he wished he could catch in a bottle, to have it by him forever.

'The land is mine and the water is mine. I can do what I like.'

5.
Into the mountain caves

Maria's mother led her down into the dark sea and until they reached the underground cavern lit by the glowing fish, where the manatee and Tomas had been together. She showed her a passageway through the rocks.

'Follow the left path as far as it goes and it will bring you out near the source of your well. It will take some time to get there but you must see for yourself what we have seen happening, all along the coastal area. There will be parts where you will have to hold your breath under water for a long time but remember, you can do it because you are part-manatee.'

Maria followed the rocky path as it climbed higher and higher. It ended at another deep lake, the lower part seawater and top, freshwater. It was dark as a starless night but a group of glowing fish had come along with her to light the way. She lowered herself into the water and found it icy from being out of the sun. She swam along the surface and soon came to a tunnel where the water reached the ceiling. She took a deep breath and dropped down, swimming as fast as she could but always glancing overhead to look for any sign of air. Eventually, she saw light up ahead and slowed her stroke. The exit to the tunnel was wide enough to allow her to breathe air once more. She stood in the water, leaning against the rock and breathed slowly and deeply.

When she felt stronger, she paddled to the edge of the opening and looked out. Everything was lit with bright lights on poles. Above and to her right there were large houses and the beginnings of other developments with fountains and what she knew must be the swimming pools Sebastian had told her about. Below and to her left she saw the valley by the sea where she lived. Out of the cliffs on either side of her and across the gulf in front of her, large rivers of water fell down the mountains towards the ocean. She traced the path of the river that filled her town's well and saw clearly the reason why it was dry. A dam had been built. It caught and trapped the water from all the rivers that ran out of the cliffs and diverted it to the new developments.

Had Sebastian lied to them? Did he know about the dam? Maria's heartbeat raced. She turned towards the tunnel, dropped into the water and made her way back through the cave system into the cavern, where her mother, once more in the form of a manatee, waited.

'They have blocked our water with a dam,' Maria said.

'They have built a marina and injure some of us with their speedboats every day,' the manatee said.

'There must be something we can do,' said Maria. 'This is not fair; there has to be some justice for the poor people of the town and for the manatees.'

With her flippers, the manatee held Maria close for a few moments before they swam back to the surface of the sea, near to the bay.

'I must go,' the manatee said. 'I will talk with the others of my kind and we will think of a solution to all of this. Will you be alright?'

Maria nodded. 'I need to talk to Tomas and Sebastian.'

'Call to me, within your mind; call and I will hear.'

The manatee turned away and dropped below the

water. Maria, being more human than not, stayed behind. As she swam away, the manatee sang one of her unusual songs. Maria listened until there was nothing but the wind to hear and made her way back home.

Back at the house, Maria found Tomas slumped in his favourite chair with his head in his hands, and she told him what she'd seen.

'Father?' she said, 'we don't have time to sit and feel sorry for ourselves. What are we going to tell everybody in the morning? They'll be expecting to find water in the well.'

'Don't you have any way at all of getting in touch with Sebastian?' he asked.

Maria shook her head.

Tomas sat back in his chair and sighed.

'I'm sorry, I don't understand this sort of behaviour at all.'

Maria's face was so confused that Tomas stood up and put his arms around her.

'It's my fault, Maria; I should have been more alert. I should have insisted I knew who he was and where he lived before letting you go out with him. I'm not good at this dad business, am I?'

Maria smiled.

'Perhaps it's me who isn't good at the daughter business,' she said. 'But it is late so let's get some sleep.'

'Maybe the well will have filled up by morning.'

'I'm not convinced that well will ever fill again.'

Next morning in the town square, people gathered. 'We have checked the well,' Bella said as Tomas and Maria approached. 'There is no water.'

Maria didn't know what to say. If Sebastian had lied to her about the water, then perhaps he had lied to her about everything. She didn't want to believe it but she couldn't deny what she had seen with her own eyes and worst of all, she didn't know how to find Sebastian to confront him.

'My olive groves are dying,' said Bella. 'Without water I will have no living to make. There will be no fresh bread for people to eat, no olive oil.'

As they waited, the townspeople became more and more agitated.

'You said you would get water, Maria. Where is it?' said one of Bella's sons.

Maria took a deep breath. 'The newcomers have built a dam to divert the water to the their developments,' Maria said.

'Why do they have to take all the water?' Bella asked

Tomas. 'Surely there's must be enough for all of us to share?'

Tomas didn't know what to say. Bella turned to Maria.

'What is your boyfriend going to do about it? He said he would look after it and make sure we had enough water.'

Maria turned around when she heard the sound of horses. Sebastian and several other men on horseback rode into the square. As soon as she saw him, Bella shouted:

'You have stolen our water.'

Sebastian said nothing until Tomas called for quiet. Maria walked over to Sebastian and some people hissed as she walked past them.

'Sebastian, you have to keep the well flowing, day and night,' Tomas said. 'You can't keep blocking our water; after all, we're paying for it and you promised you would look after it.'

Maria stared at Sebastian but said nothing.

'We own the water, Tomas,' Sebastian said. 'So you must allow us to put our peoples' needs first.'

'Shame on you,' Bella the baker shouted and others joined in.

Sebastian glanced at Maria and jumped down. Behind the horse was a cart, full to the top with plastic bottles of water. Carrying several bottles, he climbed up the market steps so that everyone could see him.

'Great news!' he said. 'I've been working hard to earn money for the town so that you can afford to buy all the water you need. I have sold the bay,' he pointed towards the sea which lapped the land where Tomas and Maria lived, 'to a developer who will build a marina there and this will bring many people to the area to buy your produce. In turn you will earn lots of money to buy water like this.' He pointed to the plastic bottles. Nobody said anything. He looked around, puzzled.

Maria suddenly pointed at him.

'Who gave you permission to sell our bay? It doesn't belong to you.'

'I bought it from The International Consortium for Continual Development, but don't worry, Maria, I put your name and your father's down as owners of your house.'

'You should have discussed it with us, Sebastian. How do you think my father can continue his fishing if the bay is full of leisure boats? They'll be building bars, cafés, places to park cars, houses, roads… and you already have a marina in the next bay.'

Sebastian ran down from the steps and put his arm around Maria, walking her away from the crowd, which had started murmuring in an unfriendly fashion. Tomas was at a loss for words.

'Darling Maria,' Sebastian said, 'your father is getting old, we'll find a place for him where he'll be warm and secure and have his own room and then you can come and live with me. Up in the town, you won't have to bother your head about wells and water or the bay.'

'Maria,' shouted Tomas. 'Are you all right?'

Maria nodded and waved to him before turning back to Sebastian.

'I'm not sure I want to marry you, Sebastian. You have told half-truths; you have diverted our water; you have sold our bay.'

'Maria, my chickadee, you don't understand. When you come and live with me, you and I will have all the water we want and I shall supply the townspeople with bottled water for as long as they need it.'

'And the bay and marina?'

'I know you don't understand commerce, and why should you, but selling it is just good business sense: Tomas is the only fisherman who works from this bay.'

'Tomas is teaching some of the young men and women from the town how to fish. He is teaching them how to make sails, how to build boats. We live by the sea, unless you and your friends destroy that as well. You're already injuring the manatees and dolphins with your speed boats...what next?'

When they heard Maria's anger, some in the crowd began shouting, 'Thief, thief, thief.'

Sebastian held up his hand.

'One moment, surely I am allowed to answer?'

The crowd quietened down and stared at him. Sebastian took his Declaration of Ownership out of his jacket and rolled it out.

'You see, it's very clear...I own the land, the water and the bay.'

People took it in turns to look at the declaration; some could read it and some couldn't but they could see the maps and the lines drawn to show how the land had been divided. Maria studied the map longer than anyone else.

'People of our town,' she said. 'It is true that all of this has been given to Sebastian and his family by the International Consortium for Continual Development...'

'It's unfair... we were not consulted...this is our land...' Bella shouted. And one by one they unfurled their own rolls of paper.

'These are our Legal Deeds for this land, dated thousands of years before yours. The land is ours! We have lived and worked here for as long as anyone can remember.'

'The land is mine,' shouted Sebastian. 'It belonged to my people, before it was yours, so the Declaration says.'

Maria stepped forward again. 'But before you took our land and before our history and your history was even written, this land belonged to different people, not your people or mine; so who are the true owners?'

'I am,' shouted Sebastian and aside to Maria he said,

'Please, don't worry your head about things that are too complex for you. When we are married you will have your hands full, with children and cooking and cleaning and you'll forget about all this nonsense. Your people have to abide by the law. Tell them Maria, they have no choice.'

Everyone stared at Maria.

'Well, Maria, what do you say now?' Bella said.

As Maria opened her mouth to speak, Sebastian pulled her to one side.

'Think about our future and our children's future and about all that travelling we will do... that's what's important. You must get your priorities right.'

Maria shook herself free of Sebastian's grip.

'We were all law abiding citizens until you changed the laws. You have stolen our water,' Maria said 'I didn't want to believe it but I have seen it with my own eyes. You have built a dam and taken all the water from the small towns and villages for your own use, squandering it and impoverishing our lands.'

'Nonsense!' shouted Sebastian.

'I swam through one of the mountain rivers,' Maria continued. 'I saw it and there are no fancy words or tricks you can use to deny it.'

Sebastian stuck out his chin and pulled his shoulders back. 'The land is mine and the water is mine. I can do what I like. So says the Declaration of Ownership.'

'There was no need for you to take all the water; there is enough for all of us. But you are greedy; you want swimming pools and fountains, while we are left with bottles of water to buy. Give us back our well and our water and leave our bay alone,' Maria said. 'There will be no marina built here, unless and until the town decides it wants one.' She moved close to Sebastian and brushed his hand with her fingers. 'If you really care about me, Sebastian, you will do the right thing. Otherwise there can be no future for us.'

The manatees sang louder and louder.

6.
What will they do?

WHILE SEBASTIAN AND MARIA ARGUED, the townspeople waited. They all knew how difficult it would be for poor farmers and fishing people to fight against the power of the new dwellers and the International Consortium for Continual Development.

Bella's sons uncoupled the cart full of water bottles from the horse and glared at Sebastian.

'You haven't paid for that water. Put it back,' Sebastian shouted.

'Leave it where it is,' said Maria. 'We'll keep this water as a down payment on what you owe us.'

'Don't be ridiculous,' Sebastian said. 'You have no

choice Maria, things have changed and from now on, you must purchase bottled water from me for all your needs. And if you don't like the idea of a marina then you must leave this area.'

Maria turned away from him. Sebastian climbed on his horse, looked back once at her and rode away with his men. The townspeople gathered bottles of water into their arms and shawls.

She watched the drooping shoulders and heads of the townspeople as they walked away. Tomas took her hand.

'They look so defeated, father. What can we do?'

He shook his head and blew out a long breath. 'I'm afraid I have no answer to that. Let's go home, while we still have one.' He took hold of Maria's upper arms and turned her to face him. 'I'm sorry Sebastian let you down.'

She sighed and kissed him on the cheek. 'No you're not, you never liked him.'

Back at the house, Tomas made a warm hazelnut drink for them both and while he went to have a rest, Maria walked to the edge of the sea, sat on a rock, turned her thoughts inwards and tried to connect to her mother. It was almost midday before she received an answer.

'I hear you, daughter…we manatees have put our minds and our long memories to this situation. We think we have found a way to help you, we will…'

As Tomas put his hand on Maria's shoulder, the connection with her mother was broken. She turned and hugged him. Time was running out and she felt sick to her stomach but now she had hope that the manatees could intervene.

'I'm, sorry father, I was fooled by Sebastian. He was different from anyone I'd ever known…but that didn't mean he was automatically better, did it?'

'No, but he was exciting, wasn't he? He had new experiences to offer…I might have fallen for him if I'd been in your shoes.'

Tomas sat down beside her and they stared at the sea, both in their different ways, silently calling for the manatees to help them.

At midday, Maria and Tomas set off for the town square. On the way there, they checked the well; it was still dry.

'You don't really think Sebastian will give us our water back, do you?' she said.

Tomas shook his head. 'No, but I don't want to give up hope.'

Once in the market square, Maria walked up the town steps and looked around at all her neighbours and friends.

'I'm sorry to say that we have come from the well and it is still dry,' she said. Everyone groaned and their shoulders drooped. Maria took a deep breath, trying to think of something she could say to soothe them. A moment later, she became very still, frowned and turned her head, as if someone was whispering in her ear. They watched her and began mumbling to each other.

'Listen,' she shouted, 'listen.'

The townspeople stopped talking and heard the rising sound of hundreds of voices singing impossible chords in pure harmony.

'What is it?' they asked Maria.

'It's the manatees, they're singing.' She paused and listened again. 'They are trying to release our water...'

'How do you know about the manatee's singing?' Bella shouted.

Maria took a quick breath. 'Because my mother is a manatee.'

The crowd fell silent.

'Now I know why you are so different,' said Bella.

Maria closed her eyes and tuned into the sound of the manatees' song and discovered she could pick out her mother's unique voice.

'Everything on this earth is susceptible to sound, Maria. We just have to find the right chords. You must sing with us...we need to create the combined voice of your people and ours in order to undo the dam.'

'How can we do that?'

'Listen to the pitch of our voices and bring yours into harmony with it. Join us, Maria, follow me at first and then find your own chords. Listen with your heart and soul as well as your ears.'

Maria closed her eyes and listened, then slowly sang along with the manatees. The singing became louder and louder; to the townspeople it was sweet, lyrical and almost unbearable. After a while, Maria found her unique voice and merged it with the others. The sound spiralled, dipped and soared until she felt sad and ecstatic all at the same time.

'Something's changing,' she called out.

Tomas jumped as the earth trembled beneath his feet. Everyone stared at the ground.

'The manatees have stopped singing,' Maria said.

'What's happening?' Bella shouted. 'What is that noise?'

'Quiet please,' Maria called out. 'I must listen.'

For several seconds there was silence. Maria, Tomas and the townspeople glanced at one another.

'Look,' Maria said, 'look.' She pointed to the top of the mountains. They all tipped their heads back and stared. It seemed like a patch of rolling dust at first but when the sun came from behind a cloud they saw that it was water, tumbling over the top of the mountains. Riding alongside it were men on horseback and in jeeps. They were throwing things into the path of the water: small trees, rocks and bushes, trying to block it, or at least divert it.

'That's Sebastian, on the grey stallion,' yelled Maria.

'They'll never stop it,' shouted Tomas.

The water suddenly curved to the right, rose up and over the stallion and knocked Sebastian off and into the water. The horse ran free and headed off towards the smaller mountain range. Sebastian's men crowded their horses together and tossed ropes to him. Each time he looked like catching one and being pulled free, the water rose higher and dragged him back under.

Soon, the din of rushing water blocked out every other sound. Blue, green and silver stars flashed off it as it rose into the air. The noise of its roar was thrilling but almost deafening.

'We must get out of the way,' Bella shouted. 'The water will carry us all off.'

Maria took hold of her father's hand.

'The water won't hurt us,' she said to Bella and the others. 'Trust me.'

Bella took hold of Maria's other hand and all the townspeople joined hands with them.

Flailing and shouting for help, Sebastian struggled to keep his head above the water as it dragged him along. His men couldn't get anywhere near him as the torrent spread wider and wider across the mountainside and dug deep into the earth.

'It's a new river,' Maria called out. 'Look, it's cutting banks on either side as it crashes down. We have a river to fill the well.'

As the flailing Sebastian got nearer, his head constantly going under the water and lifting out again, the river turned away from the bay and the town. The water carried Sebastian off on its humping back. They watched as it thundered off into the far distance. It was the beginning of a new waterway, direct from the high mountain waterfalls, which cut its way across the arid land. It unblocked the entrance to the well and filled it to the brim. The river travelled the whole length of the island, carrying Sebastian to the far ocean and beyond. He was never again seen on their land.

IRON Press is among the country's longest
established independent literary publishers.
The press began operations in 1973 with IRON
Magazine which ran for 83 editions until 1997.
Since 1975 we have also brought out a regular list of
individual collections of poetry, fiction and drama
plus various anthologies ranging from *The Poetry of
Perestroika*, through *Limerick Nation*
and *100 Island Poems*.

The press is one of the leading independent
publishers of haiku in the UK.
Since 2013 we have also run a regular IRON Press
Festival round the harbour in our native Cullercoats.
We are delighted to be a part of
Inpress Ltd, which was set up by Arts Council
England to support independent literary publishers.
Go to our website (www.ironpress.co.uk)
for full details of our titles and activities.